GLAXO

A NOVEL

HERNÁN RONSINO

**TRANSLATED FROM THE SPANISH
BY SAMUEL RUTTER**

MELVILLE HOUSE
BROOKLYN • LONDON

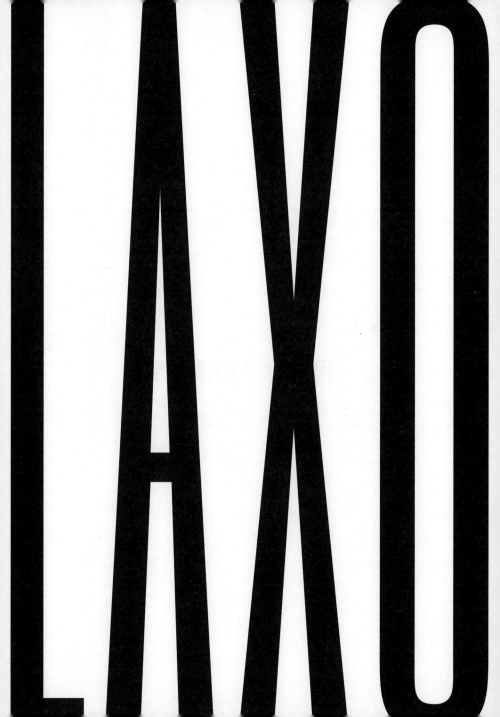

GLAXO

Copyright © 2009 by Hernán Ronsino
Originally published in Spanish by Eterna Cadencia in 2009
Translation copyright © 2016 by Melville House Publishing, LLC

First Melville House printing: January 2017

Melville House Publishing   8 Blackstock Mews
            46 John Street   and   Islington
        Brooklyn, NY 11201   London N4 2BT

mhpbooks.com   facebook.com/mhpbooks   @melvillehouse

Library of Congress Cataloging-in-Publication Data
Names: Ronsino, Hernán, 1975– author. | Rutter, Samuel,
    translator.
Title: Glaxo : a novel / Hernán Ronsino ; translated from the
    Spanish by Samuel Rutter.
Other titles: Glaxo. English
Description: Brooklyn : Melville House, 2016.
Identifiers: LCCN 2016008845 (print) | LCCN
    2016021357 (ebook) | ISBN 9781612195674 (pbk.) | ISBN
    9781612195681 (ebook)
Subjects: LCSH: Murder—Investigation—Argentina—Fiction.
    | GSAFD: Suspense fiction.
Classification: LCC PQ7798.428.O832 G5513 2016 (print) | LCC
    PQ7798.428.O832 (ebook) | DDC 863/.7—dc23
LC record available at https://lccn.loc.gov/2016008845

Design by Marina Drukman

Printed in the United States of America

1   3   5   7   9   10   8   6   4   2

The order strikes like lightning.

"Get that one, he's still breathing!"

He hears three explosions at point-blank range. At the first one, a cloud of dust shoots up by his head. Then he feels a searing pain in his face and his mouth fills with blood. The guards don't bend down to see if he's dead. Seeing his face split open and bloody is enough for them. And so they walk off, believing they've given him the coup de grâce.

—RODOLFO WALSH, *Operation Massacre*

Contents

Part I

VARDEMANN

October 1973

3

Part II

BICHO SOUZA

December 1984

29

Part III

MIGUELITO BARRIOS

July 1966

55

Part IV

FOLCADA

December 1959

73

Part I

VARDEMANN

October 1973

One day the trains stop coming. Then a work team arrives. Six or seven men get out of a truck. They wear yellow helmets. They begin pulling up the tracks. I watch them from here. I watch them work. They work until six. They leave before the workers from the Glaxo factory punch out. They leave behind a few metal drums with burning rubbish, to block off traffic. When they leave, I close the barbershop.

That's when I begin to dream about trains. About trains that run off the tracks. They sway from side to side before they fall. They destroy the tracks. Sparks fly. And then comes that noise, so shrill, just before they halt. So shrill it hurts your teeth. It moves you. Like when my razor blade scrapes over the back of the neck, and heads shudder, shoulders shudder, and it doesn't matter if it's Bicho Souza or old man Berman, their shoulders shake like the carriage of a train running off the tracks. A shiver, they call it. Then there's a warmth, on the back of the neck. And the itch of the powdered brush, sweeping the neck.

And then a primitive calm.

Now it's a warm afternoon, a Saturday. That's why nobody's working over there. Just the blackened metal drums, burning with fires that never before seemed to exist by day, with the fires burning that don't seem to be there during the day. My father and I drink yerba maté. The municipal ambulance speeds around the corner where Souza's butcher shop stands, and stops opposite the Barrios' house. With the maté in my hand, I watch from behind the door. Two doctors get out. One of them goes into the house, and Miguelito's mother greets him. The other takes out the stretcher and pushes it into the house. My father is bent over in the corner, distant and old, worn down like a bone that has been picked over. Hurry up with the maté, he says. A few minutes later the men come out, bearing the stretcher. Miguelito's mother has a fit of crying. Juan Moyano envelops her in an embrace. Once again, Miguelito Barrios is in the ambulance, on his way to the hospital.

This is the second time it has rained since the work team has been pulling up the train tracks. Now, they say, the train takes another branch line after Gorostiaga and passes by Sud, the station where before only freight trains passed through on their way from La Pampa. Endless trains. Loaded with wheat. It's the second time it has rained since the work team has been pulling up the tracks. The municipal trucks plough through the mud and are loaded with sleepers. Then they drive off, leaving behind furrows that the kids kick at as soon as they've dried, as if they were the walls of an abandoned house. But the problem is that the mud gets in everywhere. The watered-down muck sticks to everything. It covers women's shoes, the bicycles belonging to the workers at the Glaxo factory, the boots of the men who come into the barbershop and mess up the floor—despite my putting down newspaper to avoid such a disaster. It gets dragged in on the soles of shoes that sit on the footrest of the main chair, the reclining chair.

My father sweeps up the hair on the ground around the main chair, the reclining chair, painted sky blue. Three haircuts so far today. Hair from Tito Krause, Luis Aragón, and a boy who lives behind the silos piles up and melds together while my father sweeps and drags it across the mosaic tiles of black granite. It becomes a confused pile of chestnut brown and blond, mixed in with the dried mud that persists in appearing. Outside, in a clearing in the cane field, one of the men from the work team prepares a barbecue. When my father opens the door, when he goes out, bent over and slow, a broom in his hand to sweep the well-trodden path of hard, dry earth, the smell of grilling meat enters the barbershop, coming from over in the clearing of the cane field, and awakens in me a decrepit, sharp anguish. So I go out. The firm midday sun is dazzling. The summer air is ripening. I lean one arm against the doorframe. My father sweeps, with difficulty. The rest of the work team rests beneath the shade of the chinaberry trees, where there used to be a bar called the Ace of Spades. They sit on the ground, their backs against the wall, their crossed legs stretching over the brick pavement.

Then later, Lucio Montes, leaning back slightly in the main chair, talks about the fight last Sunday night, at the Bermejo Club. He talks about a guy from Mechita, a real killer, who fought Lavi, this guy Lavi from the area around Federación, and he tells me that on that night, he, Montes, didn't want to put on a bet, that he didn't go for it because he's a wimp, even though he thought he had a sure thing, and that Lavi the Kid knocked out the big guy from Mechita with one hit. Then, while Montes talks and I work, in silence, trimming the tips of his greasy hair, outside, on Souza's corner, we can see Miguelito Barrios again, holding himself up on their unfinished wall, walking with difficulty, pallid and thin just like my father. I stop, I suspend the movement of my scissors. Montes takes no notice, he keeps on talking, he says that even if Lavi looked a sorry sight, he knew, says Montes, that Lavi would knock out that big guy. He begins to angle for my attention only now, after I've spent a long while without moving the scissors through his hair. Montes watches me watching Miguelito Barrios, who now goes into Souza's butcher shop. So he's back, I say with surprise. Yes, apparently there's no cure, murmurs Montes, in a different tone, as if in fear. And then he sighs and forgets, just for a moment, about Lavi the Kid and all that business about the fight in the Bermejo Club.

pull down the shutters. The sound echoes through the houses. The metal drums, blackened, light up the piles of sleepers that will be loaded, sometime later, into the trucks from the municipal council. Crickets thrill amongst the weeds. The night advances without mercy across the countryside. It seems to enclose us. I put the padlock in place and turn the key, twice. I pull at it, before I go, to make sure it's firmly locked. I stick close to the walls, onto which the sun has beaten all afternoon, and I can still feel the heat seeping out of the bricks as I walk the twenty-metre distance home. I open the door and go in. I'm met with the sweet smell of fried onion and dull lighting. I take off the white apron I work in. (The white apron is part of my skin, I think.) My father is grating cheese onto the table. Miss Marta is in the kitchen, her back to me, stirring a bubbling saucepan. She would have put the pasta on the minute she heard the sound of the shutters. I go into the bathroom. I piss. The hard, white laundry soap darkens slightly as I scrub my hands, until the water cleans it, but still leaves behind a grey stain, like a gummy film. We sit at the table. Miss Marta tells my father not to eat any more cheese, in a scolding tone. Miss Marta serves us. I open a bottle of red wine. My father holds out his glass. Don't overdo it, says Miss Marta. I pour a glass for my father, who already has a plate of pasta in front of him. Columns of steam rise up hurriedly and fog over his glasses. How many, asks my father, while he stirs through the pasta with his fork. Six, in total, I answer, as I pull off a chunk of bread. We eat in silence.

A truck from Bustos' brickworks crashes into the row of blackened metal drums that burn until seven thirty in the morning, when the work team arrives in the rusted-out Bedford truck. Before they start work, before they put on their yellow helmets, they rub their hands together, they talk amongst themselves in a murmur. One of them, perhaps, makes a joke, makes fun of one of the others, and they laugh gently, and then they begin to extinguish the blackened metal drums, and store them away in the clearing in the cane field. Before the work team arrives, a truck from Bustos' brickworks, it seems, crashes into the row of metal drums, and some of the load of hollow bricks falls onto the road that leads to Fogón.

Miss Marta hangs a pair of my father's pants on the washing line that runs across the yard. I suck on the bitter yerba maté, sitting beneath the vines, and watch her. Her back curves over, almost on tiptoes, and with a peg in her mouth she straightens out a leg of the grey pants, dripping soapy liquid from the cuff. The work team, which had worked all morning on the edges of the tracks, now rests under the chinaberry trees of the Ace of Spades. From beneath the vines you can see the railway embankment sink through the countryside until it arrives at Route 5. From there it runs by the road for several kilometres. Beneath the sun, Miss Marta finishes hanging out the washing. She tips out the remaining soapy water from the bucket amongst the stakes holding up the green tomato plants. She comes near. She asks for some yerba maté. I serve her. She sits, and waits. Your father is asleep, she tells me, looking me in the eyes, as she pokes out her tongue slightly to sip on the maté. Miss Marta has her fingernails painted in red. She never stops looking at me, as she sucks on the straw. She sucks the maté dry. Twice she sucks it dry. She gives it back to me. Nice, she says. She gets up and walks close by me. As she brushes past, I bury my hand between her legs. Miss Marta stops. She doesn't turn around or say anything. She stops. I grab her from behind, and like always, without me asking, Miss Marta lifts up her dress, pulls down her panties and takes hold of the back of the chair, facing forward, opening her legs and bending over slightly. First I stick a finger in. Miss Marta lets out a strange gasp. Then slowly, with difficulty, I penetrate her. While she feels the stiffness entering her slowly, Miss Marta holds tightly to the back of the chair. The knuckles whiten on her hand, which, today, have fingernails painted in red.

Then I dream of trains. About trains that run off the tracks. They sway from side to side before they fall. They destroy the tracks. Sparks fly. And then comes that noise, so shrill, just before they halt. So shrill it hurts your teeth. It moves you. Like when my razor blade scrapes over the back of the neck, and heads shudder, shoulders shudder, and it doesn't matter if it's Bicho Souza or old man Berman, their shoulders shake like the carriage of a train running off the tracks. A shiver, they call it. Then there's a warmth, on the back of the neck. And the itch of the powdered brush, sweeping the neck. And then a primitive calm.

My day off, says Juan Moyano, as he obeys the order I give him, to lean forward a bit, a bit more, the head forward, and Juan Moyano obeys (like everyone else) the instructions I give him. Every two months, Juan Moyano walks into the barbershop, offers a friendly greeting and sits in the wicker chair (that is, if I'm already attending to someone else), picks up a copy of *Gráfico* magazine, crosses his legs and turns the pages slowly. When I ask him to take a seat, in the main chair, the reclinable chair, painted sky blue, he shakes my hand, I cover him with the blue smock to protect him after I've shaken it out, and he says: Same as always, Vicente, fix up the yard a bit for me. How are things, I ask him. Then Juan Moyano shakes his head, and channels the conversation towards work and politics: Things are getting serious, things are heating up. Now he tells me he's got the day off. He explains the work roster: One week of day shift, a day off, another week of night shift, a day off, and so on like that, your whole world is turned upside down all the time, Juan Moyano tells me calmly. He has been working for fifteen years in the oil factory. It's hard to sleep during the day, any little noise wakes you up. And I'm a light sleeper anyway, he says. And then, all those guys, I say, referring to the work team who right now is loading dirt onto the municipal trucks. Juan Moyano shakes his white head again and says: Don't even remind me. Then I think that Juan Moyano is a good man, a good working man. And I ask myself: Why did he get together with Miguelito Barrios's mother, after Miguelito Barrios's mother became a widow. It looks like they're going to strip the cane field, and where the tracks were they're going to build a road that will join up with Route 5, a link road, says Juan Moyano with enthusiasm. I finish the job. All done, I say, taking off the blue smock, and while I brush him off, Juan Moyano buries his right hand in his pocket and asks me how much. Same as always, I answer. And Juan Moyano pays. Before he opens the door to the street, he stops and says to me, fearfully: Vicente, Miguelito wants you to come by one of these days. Then he goes out. The white head of Juan Moyano shimmers beneath the morning sun.

It's Sunday and it's raining. Miss Marta isn't working today. Miss Marta is preparing a meal. She's looking after my father. She's looking after us. I drink maté and listen to the radio, watching the rain. The water seems to give the walls of the Glaxo factory an oily skin. And the ground turns red because of Bustos' hollow bricks, which fell off the truck a few days ago. In the beginning, when the rain started, the little flames in the blackened metal drums doubled over to survive. But the downpour really started after midday. And the blackened metal drums let off a brief and thick cloud of smoke. My father is taking his siesta. He coughs a terrible cough that echoes throughout the house. His cough becomes stranger every day, like an unknown voice. Then I see someone appear in the clearing in the cane field. It's Bicho Souza's son. He's drenched. His legs are covered in mud. He's pulling a little cart. He stops in the clearing, aiming a green shotgun, made of plastic. He throws himself to the deck, body to the ground. From behind the window of my house, I realise, as I sip on maté, and listen to Pedro Maffia play the accordion on the radio, and as the rain gives an oily skin to the walls of the Glaxo factory, turning the earth into a reddish mud, that tomorrow I will have to put up with the mud that will be dragged in and left on the footrest of the main chair, the reclining chair, painted sky blue. Then I see Bicho Souza's son, alone, moving through the rain with a green shotgun, made of plastic, playing at war and facing up at long last to those endless ghosts in the cane field.

First I hear the dry breathing of Miguelito Barrios. I hear it as I walk toward his bedroom, behind his mother. When I go in, I see a lump covered in blankets in the shadows of a room that smells like medication and disinfectant. When he sees me, he has a fit of coughing. And the foreign sound of the coughing reminds me of my father, in the house opposite, also lying down, accompanied by Miss Marta, who sits in a chair by the bed, fixing her red fingernails. Thank you, rasps Miguelito Barrios's dry voice. I just wince at him, give him a measured smile. I don't know what to say on these occasions. Even less when it's Miguelito Barrios, looking at me with sadness, trying to want to tell me something, something that hurts him as much as or even more than his coughing, which erupts unexpectedly, shaking his lungs and his body and the blankets on the bed that cover the future remains of Miguelito Barrios. But he doesn't say anything. I begin to cut his hair. The blond dry tips fall onto a blue smock I lay on top of the covers. Outside, the sounds of the work team can be heard, finishing off the job. It starts to get hot. I wonder if Miguelito Barrios will last until the end of the year. Then I think of my father and the summer, and then of Miss Marta and the summer. Miguelito Barrios grabs my arm. He's nervous. His hands are clammy, he's sweating. Don't say anything, I tell him. Don't worry. And these words hurt him more. He lets out a small whimper. He mumbles the beginnings of an explanation, the beginning of a plea for forgiveness. I impose my healthy, powerful voice over his, to erase his presence. Miguel, don't worry, I say, so much time has passed. I brush his hair, with a part to the side. I prepare him for the final goodbye. Then I leave the Barrios' house, wondering if it's right to forgive a dying man. I cross into the shade of the chinaberry trees. The work team finishes loading their tools into the municipal trucks. The cane field no longer exists, they've cleared it completely, and where the tracks once were, now there's a new road, a link road, which looks more like a closed wound. It's a road that looks like the memory of a wound in the earth that won't heal.

Part II

BICHO SOUZA

December 1984

You're no more than the reflection of the toes on your feet, I think, as I walk out of the Cinema Español, moved. I stop outside, in front of the poster for *Last Train from Gun Hill*: the young faces of Kirk Douglas and Anthony Quinn, atop an advancing train, stare back at me defiantly. I light a smoke. In the hall, a new queue forms slowly for the second screening. Somebody greets me. At last I get done with coming out of the movie (my thoughts drift away from the final scene: the showdown at the station, the train leaving, the bodies by the tracks, dead, and the look of that woman set free). I come back to reality and I discover a different town. There's been a downpour. While I was watching the film, together with eight or nine others, including Sardoni, who parked his blue Gordini on the corner of the Moulin Rouge, and the Echeverrías, they say a great big storm came down that made the temperature drop five degrees. Now the pavement is wet, it's night and it has cooled down. Then that feeling of coming out into a different town hits me in the face again, like when I was a kid and we would come out of the matinee—after spending nearly four hours in another world—we came out at nighttime, in the middle of winter, our eyes tired from watching so many movies. This brief renewal, of the town and of oneself in the town, happens again now, because I was not there when the storm blew in—I was outside of time—I was not there when the town got mixed up in that wind that would have surely blown shut the doors and the windows, that would have stirred up clouds of dust to blind the eyes. I cross the street. The lights slip off the wet pavement. I feel like I'm walking in another place, like I'm on holiday, looking for a restaurant to eat in, like there's a river nearby, a boardwalk lined with streetlights that illuminate, in stains, the edges of the river. But I go into Don Pedrín. And I sit at the table by the window. A waiter approaches. He leaves me a menu and an ashtray. The waiter looks like Anthony Quinn's son: the waiter looks like the killer. Then the Echeverrías come in, first the wife, then Echeverría himself. The wife wears sandals that leave her toes showing, and I think, again, obsessively, You're no more than the reflection of the toes on your feet.

Luque decided last week to rerun the film *Last Train from Gun Hill*. It was a surprise. He kept a copy in the cinema's archives, and according to *La Verdad*, it's one of the most moving films he's ever seen. The film premiered in 1959. And it was shown in the Cinema Español, in the spring of the same year. I went to see it with the boys from the neighbourhood. Vardemann was a huge fan of Kirk Douglas. And he loved imitating him. It was funny seeing skinny Vardemann copying Kirk Douglas's gestures and gait. We laughed in the bar at the Bermejo. The departed Miguelito Barrios, the poor thing, could walk just like John Wayne, though. And so when they got drunk, Vardemann and Miguelito Barrios set up an imaginary showdown. Vardemann went out into the street, Miguelito sat down with his back to the entrance, and when Vardemann reappeared, he was no longer the only son of the barber from Glaxo, that gawky, dull kid, now Vardemann was Kirk Douglas, and with faltering steps he closed in, struggling to hold off a smile, to tap Miguelito on the shoulder, who by then had also transformed and was now John Wayne. And so the showdown was inescapable. They stood twenty or thirty paces apart. It was amusing to see Miguelito walking just like John Wayne, bow-legged and swaying with a look of menace in his eyes. But the stiffness of Vardemann's posture was too noticeable to pass for the true movements of Kirk Douglas. It would be impossible, unless it were one of the boys in the group, for someone to tell, just by watching, that what skinny Vardemann was doing in those moments was an imitation of Kirk Douglas and not just goofing around. Then the shootout began. Vardemann loved to writhe around on the ground. Most times that's what he did. Miguelito drew and shot from the imaginary revolver in his hand, then he spun it around, blew on the end, and put it back in the holster. While Miguelito was doing that, Vardemann played at being a dead man, a wounded man dragging himself along the floor of the Bermejo (once he knocked over a table covered with bottles); and he nearly always died in the same way: he spluttered out a lament, and dedicated a few words to Nelly Sosa, his girlfriend at the time, which one of us, afterwards, had to send to her. And then he died while he let out a hoarse croak. Sometimes he'd stay down there on the ground, for a long time. We'd start chatting about any old thing, someone would put on a tango; the showdown routine was over. And so Vardemann had no other choice but to recompose himself, to go back to being skinny Vardemann, to sit in that seat in the corner against the counter in the Bermejo, and consider in silence the opinions of others, sharpening his gaze over the details. Or to chew, in a methodical manner, little cubes of cheese.

Luque says in *La Verdad*, our newspaper, that he sent his copy of the film to Buenos Aires to have a special treatment done to it, to protect it. And he says that when the film came back, it came back in colour. I have just seen, then, in the Cinema Español, *Last Train from Gun Hill*, in colour, although I recall seeing it in 1959 in colour. But that's just a memory. The queue, much longer for the second screening—there must have been twenty people—filed in gently until it disappeared behind the burgundy curtains. Sardoni's blue Gordini goes past the cinema and turns on the corner of La Farola. Behind Sardoni, Lucio Montes goes by in his pickup. As he goes by, I see that he jerks his head around to see who is in the Don Pedrín,

and when he sees me he wheels around sharply.
He parks on the corner. He fixes his clothing
a little, as he steps out, and comes towards me.
When he opens the door he winks and then
casts an eye over the rest of the room. He raises
a hand, greeting the Echeverrías. He sits at my
table. Bicho, my man, he says. He smells of
soap, and has wet hair. Have you eaten? I ask.
He shakes his head. And so I order a large
muzzarella and beer, nice and cold, with two
glasses. The waiter, the murderer of Kirk Douglas's wife, writes it down in a little notebook. It
seems like he's new. Montes says that his face
looks familiar. Have you heard the latest, he
begins, enthusiastic. I just got back from Saladillo, guess who I bumped into? His eyes are
shining, and his mouth, as Abelardo Kieffer
says, is loose. I have no idea, brother, I say, but
what the hell were you doing in Saladillo? Did
the old man send you? He says that you should
go and see him this weekend. He told me to
tell you that, if I saw you. I took the afternoon
off from the butcher shop, I went to fix up my
mother's grave, says Lucio Montes, melancholy.
But guess who I saw at the entrance to the cemetery in Saladillo? I make a gesture, purse my

lips together and shrug my shoulders, while the waiter, the murderer of Kirk Douglas's wife, sets us down a nice, cold bottle of beer and two glasses. La Negra Miranda, rattles off Montes, while I tilt the glass to let the head rise evenly. La Negra Miranda? I say, and I pass him the glass, brimming. Montes drinks it without waiting for me. He nods his head. He repeats, as he savours the beer, La Negra Miranda. And so, now that he's finished arriving—telling me how he saw La Negra Miranda in Saladillo is to have finished arriving—he takes over the table, stretches out his legs, looks out at the street and waits for me to start asking questions.

For example, if Kirk Douglas's wife, the Indian, who travels along those solitary paths in a wagon, accompanied by her son, well, if that woman, who is travelling to visit her family, if she hadn't attacked Anthony Quinn's son by beating his face with a whip, perhaps none of what happened next would have occurred. But if that is true, the film wouldn't exist either, the film that is being shown again today at the Cinema Español, in colour, and that now, surely, would be beginning its second screening with nearly twenty people inside. Here, in the Don Pedrín, Lucio Montes tells me about a ghost, because to name La Negra Miranda is like naming a ghost. I crack my knuckles on one hand. The bones pop. I followed her, says Montes, anxious. I wanted to know what she was up to, what she had done with her life all these years, he says. The waiter, Rick, the murderer, puts the pizza down in the middle of the table. Then Lucio Montes says something to him. Aren't you Salazar's kid? And the waiter, who is new, and no, has none of the cockiness of Kirk Douglas's wife's murderer, says no, that he's not from here, he's from Suipacha. He winces at us, timid, trembling, before withdrawing. But Lucio Montes is sure, he says, that he's seen that kid, he's seen that kid somewhere.

Faint drops stick to the glass of the window, blown in by a freshening wind. We eat. Lucio Montes, who chews quickly with his mouth open, says that it's drizzling. I think about Ramón Folcada, I think about Anthony Quinn and about Ramón Folcada. There is something that links them, the arrogance of power, for example, but there's also something apparently different in them, a moral limit. Someone like Pajarito Lernú, let's say, would tell me that a moral limit ceases to separate them when Anthony Quinn is questioned about the foundations of his power. You don't lay a finger on that boy, insists Quinn. And so the man who had a moral limit, who was capable of saving his best friend's life, when that guy, his best friend Kirk

Douglas, begins to question the foundations of his power, he's capable of fighting a duel if that's what's necessary to prevent it. Accordingly, I suppose Pajarito Lernú would tell me, there's no great difference between Ramón Folcada and Anthony Quinn. They stand on the same flagstones.

At first she didn't recognise me, not even by name: Montes, I told her, from Glaxo, from Souza's butcher shop. And I thought to myself that the bimbo was playing dumb to avoid me. How could she not remember me. Sure, more than twenty years have passed. But I'm almost the same, a bit fatter, but then I've always been fat. Almost the same. It's not like I changed. She was the one who was different. Oh yes. I recognised her—how can I explain it—from a tic, a little thing she did, lifting up her lips, as if to bite them, raising the bottom one. And because she seemed like her. What do I know. You can't explain these things. You recognise her or you don't. And I confirmed my suspicions when La Negra Miranda did that thing where she bites her lip, I reckon she did it when she was nervous, when she waited on the little wrought-iron tables on the pavement, and she was nervous. If I was the one who used to deliver meat to her at the bar, how could she not recognise me. Man, you're confusing me with someone else, she said to me. But I insisted: You're La Negra Miranda, Folcada's wife. And when I said it like that, when I said Folcada, she stopped, she stopped dead. She transformed. What do I know. She must bear that name on her back, I thought, just like a cross.

You're a monster, I say, and I dress him down. Montes is expecting me to say something else, that I'm interested, for example, in his story. But I'm not. I tell him he's an animal, a monster, and he sits there forcing a smile on his face that falls away, slowly, and while it falls away, his smile reveals a pair of teeth stained with oregano leaves. Hey, take it easy, what's wrong with you, says Montes. I wipe my mouth with a napkin, and I realise, as well, that Montes annoys me, the presence of Montes, his invasion, annoys me, and that's why I react how I react. There's always something behind a bad mood, an unvoiced grievance. I look out at the street, drink a little beer, and moisten my mouth. How could you talk to her like that, I say. Montes looks at me like a kid who's made a mistake, who's put his foot in it. Montes has the look of a kid who has put his foot in it. How could you put her on the spot like that, I say. And Montes goes quiet, he sits thinking, he says, What, did I do the wrong thing? You're a monster, I tell him again, an animal, the girl got scared, don't you see, she was avoiding you, she doesn't want to know anything about you, or Glaxo either. Yes, says Montes, she told me that herself afterwards. What do you mean afterwards, I say. Yes, afterwards, he says, and captures me again, the bastard, with his story.

She bought me a coffee in a shitty little bar, near the cemetery. There's something about her face, as if she had different lips, a different way of laughing. What do I know, maybe she got her lips done, who knows. She looked at me and laughed. What are you laughing at, I say. At you, the bimbo tells me. And she started laughing louder. El Monte Negro, the Black Mountain, said the stupid bimbo, teasing me. It's been a lifetime, ages since anyone called me that. It's strange when other people dig up those things. El Monte Negro, the Black Mountain, that's what Miguelito Barrios used to call me. Because one night, in a carnival parade, it was pouring down rain and I came across Miguelito on a corner, the two of us were running, and he saw me wearing a black cape and he began to laugh, and after that he began to call me El Monte Negro. What are you up to, I asked La Negra Miranda. I'm with Papelito, she says, in the circus. Come on, stop shitting me, I said. And La Negra Miranda, who has platinum-blond hair and blue eyes, but who has La Negra Miranda's tic when she gets nervous, the one where she raises her bottom lip as if to bite the other, she tells me she's serious, that one morning she couldn't stand it anymore: that night Folcada beat her, and while he beat her he told her what he had done in the clearing, he told her what Miguelito had told him, and so that very same night, she wrote a terrible letter to Miguelito Barrios, and pushed it under his door, she pushed it under before leaving, because La Negra Miranda couldn't stand it anymore, and that morning she hopped the dairy train that stopped by the doors of the Ace of Spades to load the drums from the Glaxo factory, and she said she didn't even think about it, she just jumped on the train with what she was wearing and left, she went up in smoke, she abandoned Ramón Folcada, who was sweating in the little room that opened onto the street, onto the chinaberry trees in the street. Folcada was surely snoring, while the train was taking La Negra Miranda away forever. And so this story, the story told by La Negra Miranda, is quite different from the one told by Ramón Folcada at the time. La Negrita has gone off to her mother's for a while, in San Fernando, Folcada told us, convinced—it looks like the mother-in-law might kick it at any moment. It was no effort at all for Folcada to lie, to hold up a lie. Not long ago I heard that a cancer ate up the son of a bitch and left him bare as a bone, but then some people say the commies stuck a bomb under him in Luján and blew him away. I don't know which version is true. In any case, he deserves either death. I was born again, Montes, she told me. My life went like this, she said, and flipped over one of her hands, now wrinkled and splotched on the back, by time, by the years La Negra Miranda has lived. A radical change, she told me. Then she didn't want to say any more. She asked about me, about my business, she asked me how the neighbourhood was, Miguelito's mother, she told me that one day, when she could, she would return to Glaxo to close up the wounds. But for now she told me she didn't want to know anything about all that. Then she left, alone, walking on the sealed road that leads downtown. She didn't even want me to drop her off in the pickup. Later, as I was leaving Saladillo, I saw by the side of the road that they were beginning to set up a circus tent, for Papelito's Circus. You get what I'm saying. And then I got to thinking, Bicho, about the way life changes.

Outside it's raining harder. The storm brings a fresh wind. The lights from the cinema, from the Moulin Rouge, burst against the street. Little by little, in pairs or in small groups, under umbrellas, the people who saw *Last Train from Gun Hill* in the Cinema Español, in the second screening, begin to come out. Some run to get their cars, and the women wait at the entrance. Things go by like that. Kirk Douglas, once again, leaving on a train, like La Negra Miranda, I think, each time she tells that story, which is her story. I don't know why I remember Ramón Folcada's feet, one summer evening, barefoot, hosing down the pavement. I remember his feet gnarled from rheumatism, covered in mud, a few toes twisted up above the others. You're no more than the reflection of the toes on your feet. That's how it is. Montes goes to the bathroom. His plate is full of chewed olive pits. It's five past twelve. It's already the twenty-second of December. I walk over to the public telephone in the bar. I put in a couple of tokens. I dial a number in Buenos Aires. I wait awhile, until it starts ringing, starts buzzing intermittently. When the call is picked up, the token falls, making a metallic noise, and I clear my throat, covering my free ear with my free hand to distance myself from the mingled sounds of plates and voices, there, in the Don Pedrín, and I say: Federico, happy birthday, my son.

Part III
MIGUELITO BARRIOS
July 1966

He came back yesterday. He got off the train with a shaved head and rancid skin. He looked nothing like Kirk Douglas. At that moment I could see my death clearly.

There are days when I start imagining the ways in which others will die. Because we're all going to die one way or another.

And so, sitting on the pavement in front of the house, in the Bermejo Club or while I send out the parcels from the station, I start imagining the deaths of the people I see. This idea, for years now, keeps coming back to me. It first came after seeing a film in the Savoy. And now, it comes back to me like dust filtering through the cracks in the doors and the windows, which, barely a day after the house has been cleaned, settles, this dust, once again, on the furniture, on everything. But it distracts me, I think, the insistence of this idea. If at first it terrified me, if it frightened me a little to think like that, now I'm getting more and more used to it, it clears my mind, it distracts me, imagining the deaths of others.

What I couldn't do (like the actor in the film they showed at the Savoy), what I couldn't do until yesterday when I saw skinny Vardemann get off the train, with his threadbare bag and that serene, almost hypnotic stride, was imagine my own death.

I don't agree with those who, when they choose a way to die, prefer not knowing, or hope that death takes them in their sleep, or doesn't make them suffer, as if death weren't a consequence of the life that one chose to live. I like those movies where the guys who are about to be shot don't show even the slightest bit of fear, they stand in front of the firing squad, brave, and it's the executioners, the cowards, who take aim and try to avoid the stare of the waiting man.

If my old lady heard me, or Bicho Souza, or if my old lady's new boyfriend heard me, they'd think I was crazy, or that I wanted to kill myself, or that I'd been left traumatised from the accident my old man had while breaking in a horse. But I'm not. I'm not suicidal, nor am I traumatised by my father's accident. That's why I prefer not to go around saying such things. I keep them to myself, like my own secret, to be kept only by me. I imagine it's like when a guy says he saw a flying saucer and he really did see it. I imagine you've got to have balls or be a bit crazy to tell people things like that. Because you know that no one will believe you. Or they'll treat you like you're sick. People are shallow. But we all have these ideas in our heads, I bet that everyone, even Efraín Bunge, must have ideas like that in his head, or the Germans from the Munich Club, or my mother's new boyfriend. We all have these ideas in our heads, they're like secrets, little personal treasures. That's how it is.

Once, I don't know why, the topic came up and I summoned the courage to explain these ideas to Ramón Folcada. Ever since he arrived, in '58, I've gone with Folcada every Saturday to Fogón, to polish the saddles and tack up the horses. Folcada had two horses. A dappled, peach-coloured horse that was like a dream. And a dun-coloured horse, old and gone to seed. He rode the dappled one. I rode the dun. We set off in the afternoon, through the countryside. He seemed like a foreman on a ranch, Folcada. He had a real presence on top of that dappled horse. Jugurtha, the animal was called. As soon as he recognised Folcada, Jugurtha began to nicker with delight. You say these things and no one believes you, just like the ideas I get. And that's how it came up. I told him about the idea I get, the recurring one, about the deaths of others. And Folcada listened to me, respectfully, and then he told me that sometimes people are really shallow, that people are quick to judge anybody for anything. And that you have to be careful about what you go around saying. This animal, Folcada told me, this animal would die if I stopped coming to see it. This animal, said Folcada, just like any one of us, needs a little affection.

My father was killed by a dappled, peach-coloured horse just like Jugurtha, at a horse breaking in Huergo, in 1956. My old man was a good horse breaker. That's what they said about him. That he was a good horse breaker.

He looked after Fresedo's property, in La Rica. I saw him once every two weeks, when he had a day off and appeared at the house at night. I used to wait for him, as a kid, on the pavement, I waited for his flatbed truck to round the corner at Souza's, then, when it came round Souza's corner, a deep happiness burst through me; the whole neighbourhood, in my eyes, was overjoyed at the old man's arrival. But later, when I was older, when I saw him turn in the flatbed truck, I could put things in their right places: at the end, Vardemann's barbershop, the Glaxo factory humming with machines, the neighbourhood quiet and foreign and my old man parking the flatbed truck amongst the chinaberry trees, tired, dressed in his work clothes, bearded, with rough hands. Then I recognised the nostalgia of my happiness, and I couldn't understand how it was possible that these routine actions, almost mechanical, which happened every two weeks, could have aroused in me, a long time ago, upon seeing the flatbed truck, all beat-up, and inside, driving it, a surly, dried-out man whom I called my father, a feeling similar to happiness.

After my old man died, I started to work

for the railways. In the parcels office. Alfonso Galli, a cousin of Bicho Souza, got me the job. I had to leave school, leave the white overcoat of the ninth grade and replace it with blue overalls with the insignia of Argentina Railways on the breast pocket. It's an easy job. I like it. I start at seven in the morning, half an hour before the first passenger train leaves. Then the only train before midday is the ten o'clock train. And we take care of sorting the parcels that arrive from Buenos Aires and the surrounding towns. We get everything ready, and then, in the afternoon, I head off on the delivery bike and distribute the parcels. I like delivering and dispatching packages that no one is expecting, or those that, for a while now, someone has been longing for like crazy. And there I go, knocking on the door of some house, delivering a final message. Or unexpected news.

When I've finished delivering the parcels, I head to the Bermejo. To have a drink with the boys. Before, on Fridays and Saturdays, we used to go to the movies. And then afterwards to the dance at Pileta or those other dances in the country.

But a long time ago things changed.

Things began to change one morning in '58, October of '58. The ten o'clock train came in slowly, as usual, the engine spat out thick black smoke that blocked out the view of the silos at the mills. A few minutes later, from this very train, Ramón Folcada stepped off onto the platform, a group of policemen waiting warmly for him and his wife, La Negra Miranda, who was barely twenty-eight years old and had un-forgettable legs.

That's when they opened the Ace of Spades next to my house. Folcada had been transferred as a noncommissioned officer to the town's po-lice station. And she, La Negra Miranda, who was from Buenos Aires, took care of the bar. She cooked for the workers from the Glaxo factory and for those who, gradually, heard of the place and preferred to leave the little restau-rants by the North Station and pedal at mid-day, all the way to Glaxo, to stare at La Negra Miranda's legs and fantasise about this girl who looked like none of the other girls in town.

At more or less the same time, two build-ers began to put up, on the other side of the tracks, a simple house that, by the end of 1958, was occupied by four Mormons. They always

set out early in the morning on their black bicycles with dynamos. They greeted everyone
they passed. And they came back at night,
while Ramón Folcada, for example, who wa-
tered the unsealed road before the eight o'clock
train came past, shouted some obscenity or
other at them.

A few days after moving into the house,
one of the Mormons left on the morning train.
I saw him at the station, sitting on a bench,
with two black suitcases. He was reading a
small book, which, according to Galli, was the
Bible the Yankees read. And from time to time,
the Mormon cried. Galli, while he made cal-
culations and filled out charts, told me that the
Yankees have their own bible, which lets them
go all around the world to spread the message
of their own God, Galli told me, confusedly.
But there was something concrete, something that was there for everyone to see, the
guy, the Mormon, was alone, crying, while he
read a Yankee bible, waiting for a train to take
him away from a remote town in the pampa
in Argentina.

Then, I don't know why, maybe because
of the frailty of the Mormon, so blond, so dif-

ferent from Galli, from me, from this town, crying on the bench underneath the bell, I imagined, and this was one of the first times it happened to me, I imagined this man's death. But I imagined it in a hotel, in Mercedes, at dawn, an asthma attack, the Mormon crumpling the covers on a hotel bed, in Mercedes, in the silence of dawn in Mercedes, wanting to know, for example, and unable to find out, where he was, in what town he lay dying.

The other three, however, kept on living in the little house put up on the other side of the tracks for another year; they kept on going out on their bikes early in the morning, coming back at sunset. They insisted on greeting everyone they passed, even if they didn't receive a response, and Ramón Folcada, when he saw them, kept on swearing at them under his breath, until one morning one of them was found, the shortest one, a certain Clifton Morris, that was his name, in the cane field, with a bullet in his head.

In summer, at the Ace of Spades, they used to put the little wrought-iron tables out on the pavement. At night, the tables under the chinaberry trees mixed in with the chairs belonging to my mother, and the chairs belonging to her new boyfriend, who went out to sit on the pavement, to take the air. And we were there, at the little wrought-iron tables, in the Ace of Spades, underneath the chinaberry trees. Bicho Souza and his wife, Angela, skinny Vardemann and Nelly Sosa, fat Montes and me: drinking Danubio beer and eating peanuts from their shells.

At the end of January 1959, I had to travel to Buenos Aires for some parcels. It was the first time I travelled to Buenos Aires. And to make things worse, it was for work. I was nervous. Galli prepared a map for me with the addresses and telephone numbers that I needed. He said I should relax, that Buenos Aires, until now, hadn't swallowed anyone up. On that point, our opinions differed.

When the train passed slowly by the Glaxo factory, the first thing I saw, in the distance, was the corner with Vardemann's barbershop, then, off to the side, the chinaberry trees, a little wrought-iron table, outside, next to the wall of the Ace of Spades, and, half open, the door to my house. I had the feeling that I was fleeing. But the most surprising thing was leaving behind the fixed and frozen image of that place, to see, through movement, that the world expanded once you passed the bridge on the state road, and that little portion of earth, surrounding the Glaxo factory, was nothing more than a minimal instant, almost insignificant—if it hadn't been for all the years I had lived there—on the long crossing of the journey.

It was before we arrived at Suipacha that I felt La Negra Miranda's legs brushing against mine in the wooden seat that had been free next to me.

She was travelling to her mother's house, La Negra. She was travelling alone.

Buenos Aires was for me, until then, a starving animal. A voracious, dangerous animal, like the ones in the movies on Saturday at the Savoy, those movies with huge monsters that stalk the streets and, if you're not careful, tear something off you. That's how I imagined the city, that's what I told La Negra Miranda, when the train began to reach the first clusters of buildings, and the open ground grew smaller, eaten up by the wild animal.

You're afraid, she said to me, laughing, with that voice so typical of La Negra. Then she made a proposal. She would accompany me to deliver the packages, so that I wouldn't waste time. That's what she said.

When I stepped off the train, I breathed in a strange air. They say it's the typical smell of Buenos Aires, loaded with frying, gases and damp. I got used to it little by little. We crossed the city by bus. We travelled on the subway. The thing is that by three in the afternoon I had the job done. We surfaced at the parks in Palermo. And then La Negra wanted to ride the little boats in the lake, sail around it. I recognised the place from a film. I felt like a movie actor, pedalling on the lakes in Palermo, with La Negra Miranda by my side. She was the one who went for the kiss. We ended up in bed in a hotel, opposite Estación Once.

That evening I went back alone, on the last train. A bit worried. I couldn't stop reliving that moment in the hotel. La Negra stayed in Buenos Aires for a week, at her mother's house.

When I arrived at Estación Norte, I sensed that something had changed.

Things didn't look the same. Despite everything, I kept riding horses with Folcada on Saturdays. That year, in October, my number came up for military service, and Folcada, who had contacts, got me out of it.

When La Negra came back, we began to see each other every Tuesday at siesta time, making the most of the fact that she had begun cleaning—so that no one would suspect—the little rooms at the back of the Munich Club at Estación Norte (an unnecessary job, according to Folcada). The meetings became a familiar routine, like a kind of religious act.

There's one night I can recall with particular clarity. It was during the carnival parades of '59, along the Prado Español. She went dressed as a Turkish concubine, I had a pirate costume. That night Folcada almost caught us. I was able to escape, climb the fence at the Prado Español, then run away, and while I was running away it began to rain. The rain beat down on my face. I always remember and long for that feeling, running through the streets of the town, at night, with the rain stroking my face.

Everything happened quickly: one day, in the middle of 1960, La Negra disappeared. She stopped coming to our meetings every Tuesday at the Munich. One afternoon, my mother's boyfriend handed me a letter he had found that morning underneath the door. He told me, my mother's boyfriend, that my mother wasn't aware of what was going on. It was a terrible letter. Heartbreaking. La Negra Miranda told me why she had left. Why she was abandoning everything. She told me what Ramón Folcada had done. And she couldn't believe, La Negra Miranda, how I could be capable of taking part in such a thing. She told me that she preferred to run away rather than live with vultures. She called me a vulture, La Negra Miranda. Then I began to listen to what Folcada said, every time someone asked after her; Folcada said that she had gone to her mother's house, in Buenos Aires, because her mother was liable to die at any moment. I awaited her return more and more anxiously as each day passed. I even planned, after a few weeks, a trip to Buenos Aires to find her, a trip I never took. And then after a few months we awoke in the neighbourhood to find the Ace of Spades closed. A few days passed and nothing changed. To this day we haven't heard a thing about Ramón Folcada or La Negra Miranda. We just know, from what we can see, that the Ace of Spades is, as each day passes, an abandoned building, with a wrought-iron bench on the sidewalk that rusts over a bit more each time it rains, that is sinking, slowly, into the ground, and next to the wrought-iron bench—that's what we can see, because how could we not notice—clumps of weeds and creeping vines slip between the cracks, in the joints in the walls. That's what the Ace of Spades, inevitably, for years now, has been transforming into.

But the most important thing happened yesterday. And I have to tell it. He stepped off the train with a shaved head and rancid skin. He didn't look like Kirk Douglas at all. At first I didn't recognise him, I saw a skinny guy, tall, who was watching me from the end of the main platform, with his fists clenched by his sides. Smoke from the train swirled around us. It looked like a scene from some Western: I re-membered *Last Train from Gun Hill*, but skinny Vardemann didn't look like Kirk Douglas. And when the platform emptied out, I recognised him. They let him out early, I thought. He still had more than five years left. Vardemann drew an imaginary revolver, like we used to do in the Bermejo—I was John Wayne, and he'd be a poor imitation of Kirk Douglas—and he shot me. Then he gave a hint of a grimace. He blew on the tip of his finger. And he walked off by the railway track, with that serene stride, almost hypnotic. This time he didn't throw himself to the ground, he didn't want to play dead. This time, skinny Vardemann was playing another part, the part of the executioner or the avenger. And that's how it is: I have to tell it. And so, ever since yesterday, and I'm not lying, I can see clearly the possible form that my death might take.

Part IV

FOLCADA
December 1959

Someone's fucking La Negra. I'd bet my last dollar on it. That's how it is. I saw something at the carnival parade. I felt the sting. Doubt, they put the doubt in my mind. Ever since, La Negra has been playing dumb. I never said anything to her. I don't want to show my hand. I want her to trap herself. I have her in my sights. Oh, yes. I have her in my sights. As soon as she puts her foot in it, I'll break her neck. I saw something at the carnival parade. And that's how I know it's some brat. A kid. I saw them from afar. And they were even disguised, in costumes. In Jugurtha's war there were men who wore disguises. That's what it says in the book that Lieutenant Segovia gave me one night at the police academy. I was on the late watch. The Lieutenant showed up in his pyjamas. This is for you. And he left. He gave me this book about Jugurtha's war. He left it with me because he knows that I like history. The great adventures. Stories about warriors. And so I set myself to devouring the book, which has about a thousand pages. Now I know it almost by heart. And in one scene, in the war, some of Jugurtha's soldiers in disguise betray one of the generals from the enemy army. A trap. Something like that. Betrayal is the foundation of power. That's how history advances. I see them and I think of the South Seas, says Jugurtha, astride his horse, as he watches how the enemy army—the Romans are the enemy—how they wait, and Jugurtha doesn't know that this enemy army will end up killing him. You watch me, Jugurtha says to his enemies, and I think of the South Seas. That's why you might betray me. Behind a disguise, always, brewing slowly, is a gentle betrayal. That's why you can't deny that for a while now La Negra Miranda has been different. Distant. She looks at me, and she doesn't smile like before. In fact, when she sees me she bites her lip. And La Negra bites her lip when she's nervous.

She's hiding something. In the Prado Español, I saw her with a guy. I couldn't see what costume he had, the guy. But they planted the seed. They left me the doubt. And that's what grows inside me every day. It eats me up. The doubt. Because she's hiding something from me. What's more, now people are talking about the whole Suárez business. I can't remember how I heard about it. What I do know is that they haven't named me. They tell how things are. It pisses me off how they make everyone out to be little angels. They're not all little angels. There was a revolution. We stopped a revolution. And we did it how we had to do it. Sure, something went wrong, because afterwards they sent us all over the place. I chose this town. As a kid I came here to my grandparents' place in the country. My grandparents died and they sold the property. I always had a fond memory of this town. I learned how to ride in this town. That's why the first thing I did, when I arrived, was buy a horse. I named him Jugurtha. He's a dappled, peach-coloured horse. I always liked that type of horse. Jugurtha had a dappled, peach-coloured horse. He fought astride that animal. When I saw La Negra Miranda's legs, I thought of Jugurtha's horse. I don't know why. Could there be a logical answer? I saw her legs at a dance put on by the fire brigade in La Boca: I saw her legs, and I thought of Jugurtha's horse. And I bolted too, just like a horse, when I saw her legs. An infernal dark-haired beauty. La Negra reminds me of the actress from *La morocha de Abasto*. Not because they look alike, but because of her attitude. Sometimes I whisper that to her during siesta. There's nothing better than being naked with La Negra. During the siesta. In summer. But during any siesta. In summer, it's better, with the fan turning and the curtains half closed. And us barely covered by a clean, fresh sheet. It's the best thing there is. Rubbing against La Negra's body. Touching her legs. While you hear the birds outside. You can hear kids talking in low voices. And they run along with their slingshots and pockets full of chinaberries. And you can hear too, while we're rubbing against each other in bed, La Negra and I, you can hear Jugurtha snorting. His tail shooing away a fly, tied to a chinaberry tree. All that comes from outside. While the fan cools us down. And La Negra and I grind against each other, naked. It's the best thing there is. The best. Tita Merello, I tell her. You're like Tita Merello in *La morocha de Abasto*. And she doesn't like it. She pretends to be offended. She says Tita Merello is ugly. But that's what La Negra is like. A woman like her with a body like that in this town. Of course she attracts attention. That's why it's so easy for someone to fuck her. And it's not crazy to think that La Negra would fuck around with some kid. Some kid who picks up La Negra and fucks her like you'd fuck Marilyn Monroe. A real woman like La Negra. And La Negra must like being fucked by a kid. And that the kid would fuck her with a fantasy like that in his head. As if she were Marilyn Monroe. That must get La Negra hot. And that must get the kid really hot. The kid must be in love. That's how it is. I'd bet my last dollar on it. And so a kid who is in love with her is fucking La Negra and fucks her like she's Marilyn Monroe. That doesn't mean the kid fucks her well. Because I fuck La Negra well. La Negra howls with pleasure during siesta. We rub on each other real sweet. And the fan cools us down. And barely a freshly washed sheet touching our bodies. And La Negra howls. La Negra likes how I fuck her. What I'm talking about is something else. That La Negra must like fucking the kid. Not because the kid fucks her well. But surely because the kid fucks her like she's Marilyn Monroe. And that's how the kid falls in love. Who could fall in love like that? Who could fuck La Negra Miranda like that? Anybody. But it's a kid from the neighbourhood, for sure. I don't reckon it's Miguelito. Miguelito has a head full of ghosts. He tells me he thinks a lot about death. He tells me about his father. He describes, every time we go riding, the way a dappled, peach-coloured horse that looked like Jugurtha threw off his father while he was breaking it in. It seems like he was a real son of a bitch, the father. That's what they say about him. That Miguelito's father was a real son of a bitch. But that means that Miguelito could never fuck La Negra like that. And so who? Bicho Souza? I don't think so. He's about to be a father. And I know that has nothing to do with it. But he's more of an expressive type. An artist. The guy who fucks La Negra Miranda like she was Marilyn Monroe, and falls in love with her, would have to be more of a reserved type. A closed-off kind of guy. A guy who jerks off looking at a porno mag. Something like that. And so when the kid comes across La Negra Miranda's legs, he can't help but see her as if she were one of those photos that he looks at while he jerks off. That's how it is. I'd bet my last dollar on it. That's why Bicho Souza isn't the guy. I'm not ruling anyone out. But he doesn't fit the profile. That leaves two. Both of those two fit the profile. Lucio Montes is one of them. A butcher. Fat. No known girlfriends. An ogler. He turns around to check out the arse of any girl who passes. He's a hot tip. He has all the characteristics. And the other one is the barber's son. Vicente Vardemann. That guy has a girlfriend. But he also has a dark aspect. He's tall and skinny. He has sweaty hands. He's reserved, sad. He's also a candidate. If they asked me to choose, I'd have to say Montes. But sometimes the most obvious choice is the wrong choice. And so it could be either of them. And then if you consider La Negra Miranda. If you think about how it could be possible that La Negra Miranda gives either of these guys the time of day. I answer that with what I said earlier. What La Negra likes is for the kid to fuck her thinking that he's fucking a real woman, an unattainable woman. Impossible. And she'd like that, because the kid must tell her that. While he fucks her, he must whisper those sorts of things in her ear. He must tell her that he's in love. Because this kid fucks her the same way he jerks off to a photo of Marilyn Monroe. The same way. The kid is a closed-off guy. Dark. Dangerous, I'd say. That's why I need someone. An informant. Maybe Miguelito. Because he's the only one I'm sure it isn't. And besides, I trust him. One day I make him an offer, in Fogón. We're riding through the countryside. He tells me about his father's death. He tells me he sees dead people. I could tell him, but I don't, that in reality he sees his dead father, falling from a dappled, peach-coloured horse while breaking it in. That's what Miguelito sees, when he sees dead people. But one Saturday we're riding and it's cloudy and Miguelito is all upset, talking to me about death, and I tell him I can save him from the draft, because Miguelito got a really high number, number 931, and with that number, I tell him, you'll be going to the south. For sure. And then I make him an offer. And Miguelito accepts even before I tell him what it is. And he accepts because the kid's scared, he's afraid. And I also make him the offer because I've gotten to like the kid. And I do it, you could say, for the country. A kid like him shouldn't be a part of Argentina's army. A kid who's afraid and sees dead people everywhere can't be a soldier. And so I also do it for that. I promise to save him from the draft if he finds something out for me. Of course. Because Miguelito hasn't got a fucking clue that La Negra is cheating on me, well, that some kid is fucking La Negra. He says yes. He says no problem. That whatever I want to know he'll find out if it means dodging the draft. He says he's thankful, that he'll always be thankful to me. And that I can count on him for whatever I need, whenever I need it. Miguelito Barrios is a grateful kid. I don't like grateful kids. They're blind. How is it possible that a grateful kid like Miguelito came from a father like Miguelito's father, who is said to have been a real son of a bitch, an arsehole, and from an old slut like Miguelito's mother, who as soon as her husband was dead, shacked up with that loser Moyano, that Juan Moyano. I don't have the answer. These things happen. One of these days, La Negra will give me a son. A real son. I won't have to save the son La Negra gives me from national service. It won't be necessary. Because the son La Negra gives me will be a true general. He'll have balls and he'll be proud of Argentina's army. Argentina's army will be proud of the son La Negra Miranda gives me. And so I tell Miguelito that I'll save him from the draft, that I'll have my contacts make some moves, that's what I tell him, and the kid's eyes open wide. What would Miguelito imagine when I tell him that it will be no big thing to have my contacts make some moves? Would he think of a chessboard? Is that what Miguelito would think? Me, for example, moving some pieces around on a chessboard. These contacts I have. And that's how I'll save him. But what does he have to find out, for me to save him, having my contacts make a move. And Miguelito doesn't ask me this, because he's a grateful kid, that is, a blind kid. Just a quick phone call, I tell him. What will he think then? Whatever you need, the kid tells me. Then I pull on the reins. Jugurtha halts. I look the kid in the eye. I tell him, I'll save you if you tell me who's fucking La Negra. The kid goes white. Then he looks away. He gazes into the distance, to the end of the track. He looks into the scrub. His hands are shaking. The kid must be afraid, because he must know who's sleeping with La Negra. He's as white as cheese. I tell him: Someone from your gang, one of your friends, is fucking La Negra. I have proof, I say, to put the screws on him. The kid stays quiet. He doesn't know what to say. He doesn't react. Or rather, he reacts with fear, with silence. And so I pile it on: You tell me who it is and I save you. Easy. Simple. I tell him: It's either Montes or Vardemann. You find out for me. And when I give him the names, he looks at me viciously, like when you solve the mystery of a riddle. Like when one guy hits the nail on the head, and the other, who knows where the nail is, can't say anything yet. And then figuring out the secret moves him, strikes him. Because, of course, I hit the nail on the head. I named Montes and Vardemann. It's one of those two. If you ask me, because of the profile, it's Montes. But you never know. Before finishing, I clear things up. Miguelito, I tell him, I'm looking for a bond of confidence, I'm looking for this to stay a secret. I trust you, I say. The kid replies, with fear. A bit less pale. A bit less stupid. That's the way things are. And so the days go by. Three or four days pass. Miguelito goes around unsettled. He comes and goes, nervous. The kid has to betray someone. If he wants to get himself out of national service, he has to sell out one of his friends. In the evening they sit at the tables on the pavement. And I keep watch over them. They talk. They laugh. But Miguelito searches for silence. He's looking for an answer to give me. And that weekend, astride the fat old dun-coloured horse, he tells me he knows who it is. He looks the other way when he tells me who's fucking La Negra Miranda. And when he finishes telling me who's fucking La Negra Miranda, he bolts off, on the horse, on the old dun. In a rage, the kid took off. And I understand him a little, but that's the way things are. And so, now that I know who's fucking La Negra, I begin to think. I look for a plan. I watch him, the kid who's fucking La Negra, in the Ace of Spades, sitting with his friends. The brat doesn't know that I know. Miguelito isn't at that table. Miguelito, I hear, is bedridden, with a cough. I lie awake all night planning how to attack. Before the sun comes up, I head out into the countryside. I need to ride Jugurtha. Take in the fresh air. Clear my head. But when dawn starts to break, I decide to go back. I go back with Jugurtha, confused. I tie the animal up amongst the chinaberry trees. Everyone's still asleep. I drink maté in the shade. Jugurtha is unsettled, surely because of how hot it will be later. And then at around seven, I see him go out. He leaves the house on his bicycle. He passes by me and greets me. When the Mormon greets me, things fall into place. I call him over. I offer him some maté. I start to chat with him. The Mormon doesn't understand a word. I don't understand what the Mormon says. I tell him to wait. And I go inside. Inside, I look for the *matagatos*, the single-shot pistol. And when I come out, with the pistol hidden in my pants beneath my shirt, I see the Mormon sitting down beneath the chinaberry trees, happy, with the maté in his hand. He grins at me, that Mormon son of a bitch. And then I tell him to come with me. And the Mormon comes with me. Because he has no idea what he, when he greeted me, stirred in my mind. The idea he just gave me. And so the Mormon, who trusts me, and who hasn't got a fucking clue what just popped into my head, follows me. We walk over to the cane field. The Mormon comes along with his bicycle. I go a few steps ahead. Then we're deep into the cane field, from where you can no longer see the street, or the Glaxo factory (you can just see the tip of the smoke-stack). Where you could even say that silence reigns. Where the thrumming of the town dies away. And so when we're there, I look at the Mormon, who is short and a little fat, and who looks back at me, happy. And there's a name written on the pocket of his white shirt that says CLIFTON MORRIS. That's his name, that fucking Mormon. Then I make him put down his bicycle. And when the Mormon puts down his bicycle, I hit him in the face. My little fin-ger hurts a little when it smacks into his face. The Mormon, who wasn't expecting a fist to the face, because he didn't have a fucking clue that just by greeting me he'd given me a plan—when he, the Mormon, receives the whack I give him on his mug, he falls on his arse. Now his face is disarranged. Surprised. *What, what,* says Clifton Morris. And when he's there, fallen on his arse in the middle of the cane field, then I point the pistol at him and I begin to speak. Because it's still early. Because there are still twenty or thirty minutes before the first train comes past. You don't have anything to do with La Negra, I begin to tell him. You have nothing to do with La Negra Miranda, you Mormon son of a bitch. I talk to him, I keep him occupied. You're a dirty Yankee spy, I tell him. From the CIA, you're from the CIA, you are. I didn't have a plan, until I saw you. So now we're going to wait for the train. And you know what, you fucking Mormon. When the train goes by, I won't make a mistake like the mistake I made that night in the dump at Suárez. And because I made a mistake that night in the dump at Suárez, that dirty Peronist is still alive. And now there's a book. In that book I'm not named. It tells how he got away. He escaped the massacre. Because they're calling it a massacre. But what that son of a bitch doesn't know is that he escaped because I made a mistake. And for that mistake I'm here now, in this shitty town. Once upon a time I loved this shitty town. But now it's just a shitty town. You know what, you Mormon son of a bitch? I'd like to know what the fuck you're doing here. You're here for sure because you're a spy, from the CIA, that's what you are, you fucking Mormon. Because I didn't have a plan. And then at half past seven, the train goes by. The first train of the morning. The sound of the train covers the noise of the bullet I put in that Mormon's head. This time I make no mistake. The little man goes still, with his head buried in a pool of blood. I've always wanted to kill a Yankee. A fucking Mormon. They're Yankee spies. The Mormons are Yankee spies, from the CIA, that's what they are. And then, at eight, I go into the barbershop. I am, of course, the first customer. Old man Vardemann looks after me, listening to the radio. I ask him to shave me. The old man gets me ready. And before he shaves me, he goes into a little room looking for something, something that he mumbles about, old man Vardemann. I take advantage of this and hide the pistol in a drawer of the dresser that's underneath the mirrors. The barrel's still hot. The tango spluttering out of the radio is called "Pichona mía," and it's sung by Livio Brangeri. Afterwards I head out, clean-shaven, smelling of cologne, and the morning is already alive: on Souza's corner there's a group of people. Bicho Souza gets out of a car. He embraces his father. When he sees me crossing the street, he greets me. He's happy. Bicho Souza's wife has a baby in her arms. That means Bicho Souza's kid was born. And the Souza family is happy. They welcome the baby home. Behind the Souza family, who are happy, La Negra Miranda, barefoot, strokes Jugurtha's flank. All that's left to do now is make a call, I think, while I walk towards the chinaberry trees, where Jugurtha is tied up, where La Negra Miranda stands, barefoot, stroking Jugurtha's flank. All that remains now is simple: wait for the squad cars to come by and arrest skinny Vardemann, for murder.

About the Author

HERNÁN RONSINO was named one of the "25 Best Kept Secrets in Latin America" by the Guadalajara International Book Fair. He was born in Chivilcoy, a small town in Argentina's pampa, and currently teaches at the University of Buenos Aires. *Glaxo* is his first book to be translated into English.

About the Translator

SAMUEL RUTTER is a writer and translator from Melbourne, Australia.